ANGUS - CULTURAL SERVICES
D0337148

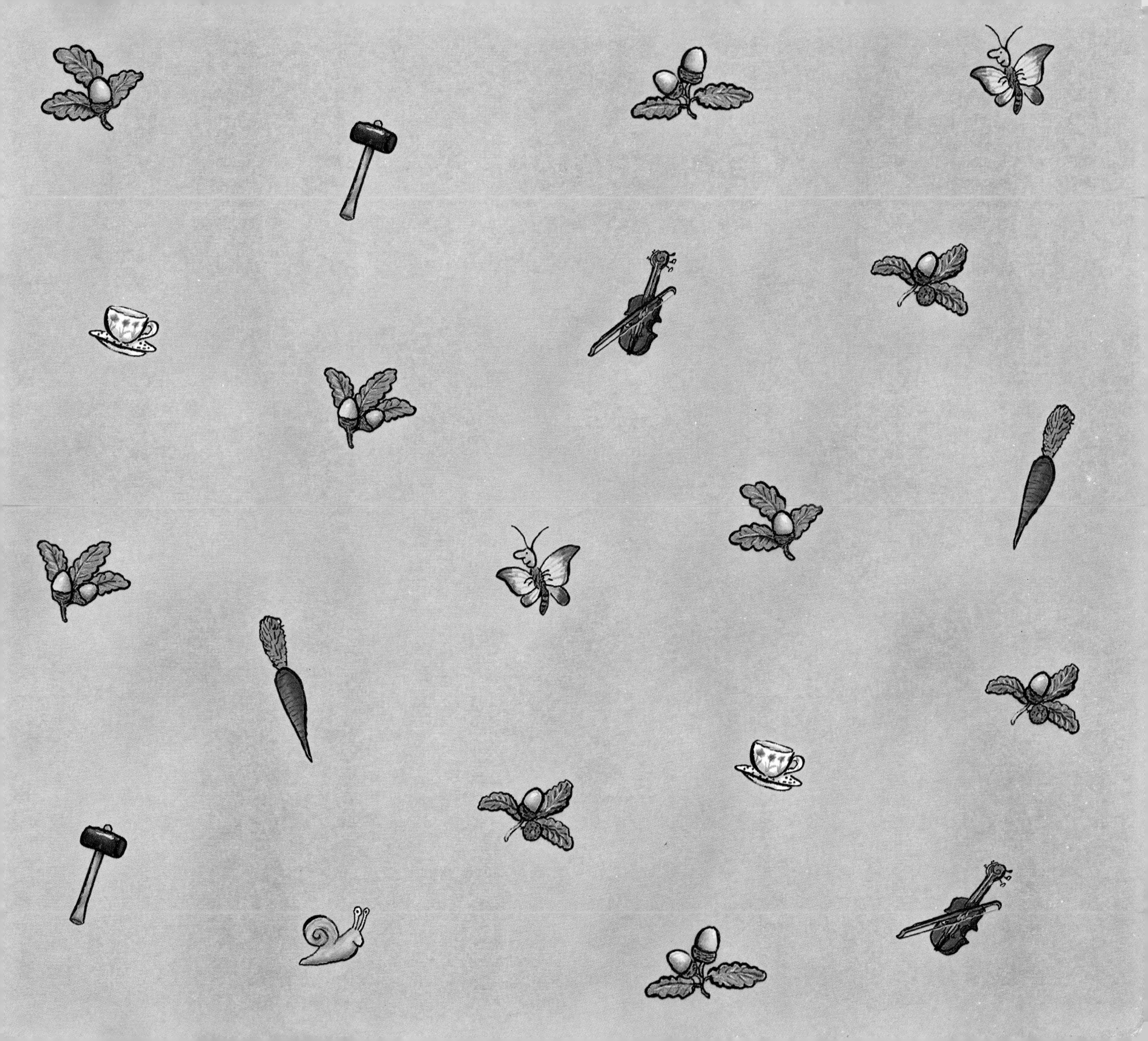

First published 2000 by Macmillan Children's Books
This edition published 2003 by Macmillan Children's Books
a division of Macmillan Publishers Limited
20 New Wharf Road, London N1 9RR
Basingstoke and Oxford
Associated companies throughout the world
www.panmacmillan.com

ISBN-13: 978-0-333-98738-4
ISBN-10: 0-333-98738-1

A CIP catalogue record for this book is
available from the British Library.
Printed in Malaysia

7 9 8 6

Tales from Acorn Wood

Rabbit's Nap

Written by Julia Donaldson   Illustrated by Axel Scheffler

MACMILLAN CHILDREN'S BOOKS

Rabbit's feeling sleepy.
She curls up in a chair.

Tap! Tap! Who's that?
Oh dear! It's Builder Bear.

Where can Rabbit have her nap?
The window seat looks nice.

Bang! Clash! Who's that?
Oh no! A band of mice.

Rabbit's in her deckchair.
A doze would be so good.

Whack! Crack! Who's that?
It's Fox - he's chopping wood.

"A shady tree!" says Rabbit.
"The kind of spot I like."

Ting-a-ling! Who's that?
It's Tortoise on his bike.

Poor tired Rabbit goes back home.
She yawns and rubs her eyes.

Rat-a-tat! Who's that?
"Your friends with a surprise!"

"Hush-a-bunny! Tra-la-la!
We'll sing you off to sleep!"

Zzzzz! Zzzzz! What's that?
Shall we have a peep?

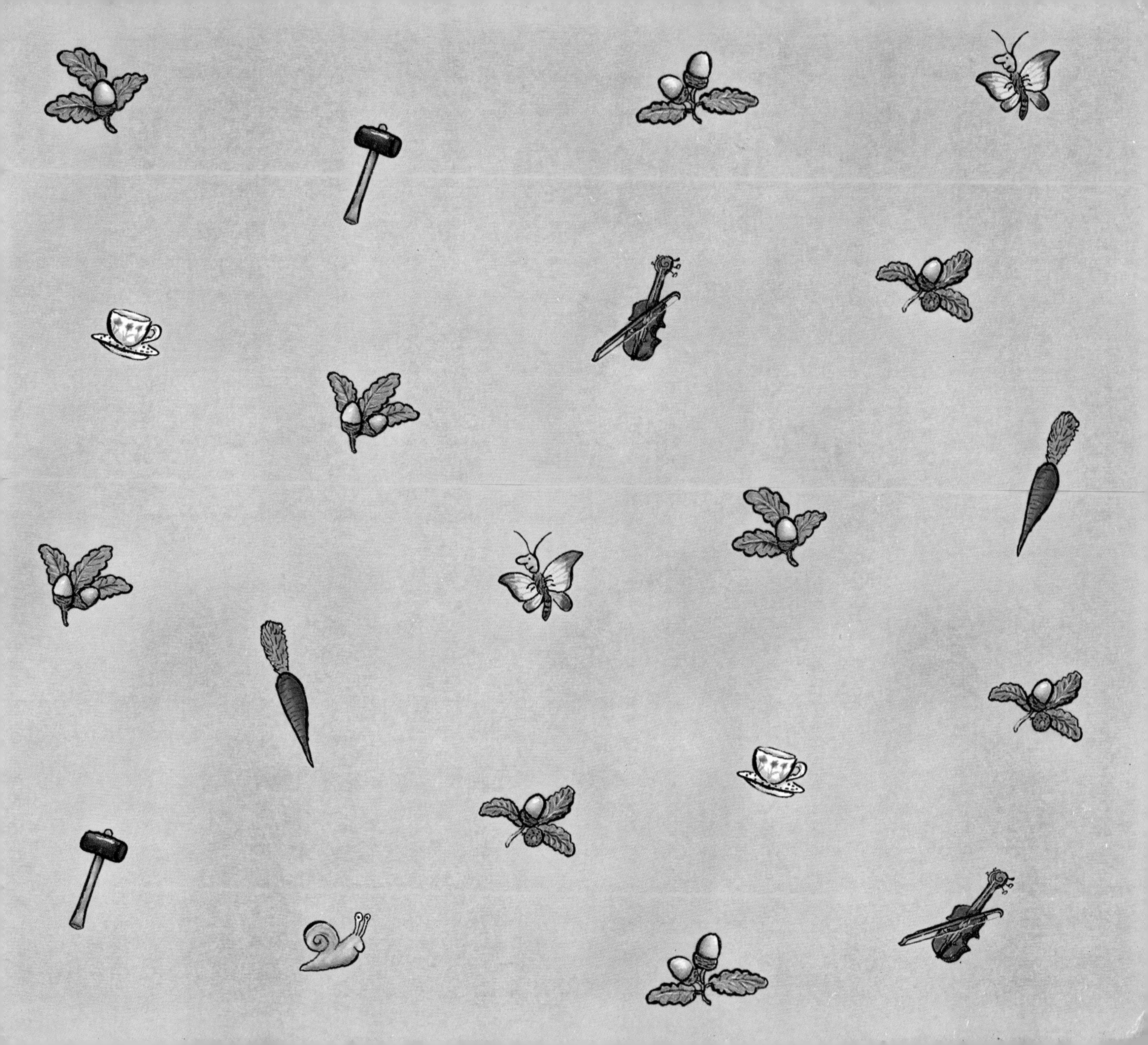